Piano/Vocal/Guitar

D1524467

THE NEW BEST OF WILLIE NELSON

CONTENTS

TAKE IT TO THE LIMIT

Words and Music by
DON HENLEY, GLENN FREY
and RANDY MEISNER

IF YOU CAN TOUCH HER AT ALL

Words and Music by
LEE CLAYTON

1. Fun - ny_____ a wom - an_____ can come on so wild and free,_____
2. One night_____ of love _____ don't make up for six nights a - lone,_____
3. Right_____ or wrong_____ a wom - an can own an - y man,_____

Yet in - sist I don't
I'd rath - er have
She can take him in -

watch her un - dress or watch her watch me.
one than none 'cause I'm flesh and bone.
side her and hold his soul in her hand.

SPANISH EYES

Words by
CHARLES SINGLETON and
EDDIE SNYDER

Music by
BERT KAEMPFERT

9

WHISKEY RIVER

By
JOHNNY BUSH

ANGEL FLYING TOO CLOSE TO THE GROUND

Words and Music by
WILLIE NELSON

15

WITHOUT A SONG

Words by
WILLIAM ROSE and
EDWARD ELISCU

Music by
VINCENT YOUMANS

MONA LISA

By
JAY LIVINGSTON and
RAY EVANS

Ab Eb
smile to tempt a lov-er, Mo-na Li-sa, or is this your way to hide a bro-ken
3
mf
Ab Abm Eb Bb7
heart? Man-y dreams have been brought to your door-step. They just lie there, and they
mp
Eb Eb7 Ab Eb
die there. Are you warm, are you real, Mo-na Li-sa, or just a
Bb7 1. Eb 2. Eb
cold and lone-ly, love-ly work of art? Mo-na art?
rall.

SEVEN SPANISH ANGELS

Words and Music by
EDDIE SETSER and
TROY SEALS

24

Verse 2:
She reached down and picked the gun up
That lay smokin' in his hand.
She said, "Father, please forgive me;
I can't make it without my man."
And she knew the gun was empty,
And she knew she couldn't win,
But her final prayer was answered
When the rifles fired again. *(To Chorus:)*

WHY DO I HAVE TO CHOOSE

Words and Music by
WILLIE NELSON

Why do I have to choose _____ the ev-'ry-bod-y blues, _____ the walk-a-round-and-cry-the-blues? _____ — Well, dar-ling, I re-fuse. _____ 1. Love is hard to

26

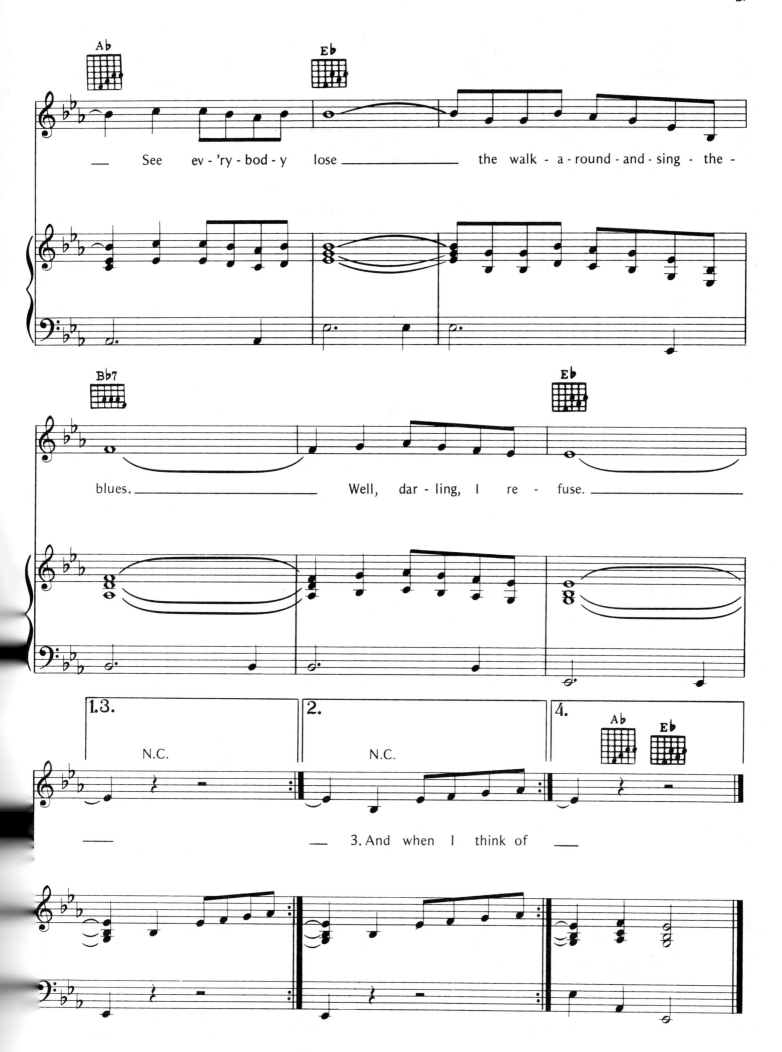

HELP ME MAKE IT THROUGH THE NIGHT

Words and Music by
KRIS KRISTOFFERSON

STAY ALL NIGHT (STAY A LITTLE LONGER)

Words and Music by
TOMMY DUNCAN

1. Can't go home__ if you're go - in' by the mill__ 'cause the bridge__
2.5. *(See additional lyrics)*
3.4. *(Instrumental)*

__ washed out__ at the bot-tom of the hill. The big creek's up, lit -

tle creek's lev - el; plow__ my corn__ with a dou-ble shov-el. You got-ta

Chorus:

stay all night, stay__ a lit-tle long-er; dance__ all night,__ dance__

er.

(Play 12 times)
D.S. al 5th ending

Coda

2. Now you ought to see my blue-eyed Sally;
   Lives way down on Shinbone Alley,
   And the number on the gate
   And the number on the door,
   Next house over is a grocery store.

   (To Chorus:)

3. *Instrumental*

4. *Instrumental*

5. Take your mama, stand her on the head.
   If she don't like this, can you feed her cornbread?
   Gals around big creek about half drawn;
   Jump on a man like a dog on a bone.

   (To Chorus:)

ON THE ROAD AGAIN

Words and Music by
WILLIE NELSON

Verse 2:
On the road again.
Goin' places that I've never been.
Seein' things that I may never see again,
And I can't wait to get on the road again.
(To 2nd ending)

BLUE EYES CRYING IN THE RAIN

By
FRED ROSE

HEARTBREAK HOTEL

Words and Music by
MAE BOREN AXTON,
TOMMY DURDEN and ELVIS PRESLEY

42

Verses 3 & 4:
Instrumental solo

Verse 5:
Well, the bellhop's tears keep flowing,
The desk clerk's dressed in black,
They've been so long on Lonely Street
They'll never, never, never get back.
I've been so lonely, baby, I get so lonely baby,
I get so lonely I could die.

Verse 6:
So, if your baby leaves you,
You got a tale to tell,
Just take a walk down Lonely Street,
To Heartbreak Hotel.
I get so lonely, baby, I get so lonely, baby,
I get so lonely I could die.

Verse 7:
Instrumental solo

CITY OF NEW ORLEANS

By
STEVE GOODMAN

45

I'll be gone_____ five hun - dred miles _____ when the day _____ is

done.

2. Dealin' card games with the old men in the club car,
   Penny a point ain't no one keepin' score.
   Pass the paper bag that holds the bottle;
   Feel the wheels grumblin' 'neath the floor;
   And the sons of Pullman porters, and the sons of engineers
   Ride their father's magic carpet made of steel.
   Mothers with their babes asleep are rockin' to the gentle beat
   And the rhythm of the rails is all they feel.

3. Night time on the City of New Orleans,
   Changin' cars in Memphis, Tennessee;
   Halfway home, we'll be there by mornin',
   Thru the Mississippi darkness rollin' down to the sea.
   But all the towns and people seem to fade into a bad dream,
   And the steel rail still ain't heard the news;
   The conductor sings his songs again;
   The passengers will please refrain,
   This train's got the disappearin' railroad blues.

MY HEROES HAVE ALWAYS BEEN COWBOYS

Words and Music by
SHARON VAUGHN

50

LOOK WHAT THOUGHTS WILL DO

By
LEFTY FRIZZELL, DUB DICKERSON
and JIM BECK

1. 4. Once, I thought I loved just
2. *(See additional lyrics)*
3. *(Instrumental)*

you, and I thought____ you____ loved me, too, but to-

To Coda

day you say we're through.____ Just look what thoughts will do.__

just look what_____ love will_____

do._____

2. And if, within your future years,
   Your new love should bring you tears,
   And you'll think of me, I'm sure,
   But those thoughts won't help you, dear.
   Once I thought I loved just you;
   And I thought you loved me, too,
   But today you say we're through.
   Now, just look what thoughts will do.

ALL OF ME

Words and Music by
GERALD MARKS and
SEYMOUR SIMONS

OLD FRIENDS

Words and Music by
ROGER MILLER

58

2. Old *Instrumental Solo*

Repeat ad lib. and fade

Old Friends - 4- 4

FADED LOVE

Words and Music by
BOB WILLS and
JOHNNY WILLS

look at the let-ter that you wrote to me;

2. (See additional lyrics)

it's you that I'm think -ing

of.   As I   read   the

lines   that to me were so sweet,   I re-

2. As I think of the past and all the pleasure we had,
   As I watch the mating of the dove,
   And it was in the springtime that we said goodbye.
   I remember our faded love.

(To Chorus)

IF YOU'VE GOT THE MONEY, I'VE GOT THE TIME

By
LEFTY FRIZZELL and
JIM BECK

66

I've got the time._____

3. We'll go honky tonkin';
   Make ev'ry spot in town.
   We'll go to the park where it's dark
   And we won't fool around.
   If you run short of money,
   I'll run short of time.
   You got no more money, honey,
   I've no more time.
   If you've got the money, honey,
   I've got the time.
   We'll go honky tonkin'
   And we'll have a time.
   Bring along your Cadillac;
   Leave my old wreck behind.
   If you've got the money, honey,
   I've got the time.

A GOOD HEARTED WOMAN

Words and Music by
WILLIE NELSON and
WAYLON JENNINGS

ALWAYS ON MY MIND

Words and Music by
WAYNE THOMPSON, MARK JAMES
and JOHNNY CHRISTOPHER

HEARTACHES OF A FOOL

Words and Music by
WALT BREELAND, PAUL BUSKIRK
and WILLIE NELSON

boy I would walk_____ through_ the val - leys,

2.3. *(See additional lyrics)*

and gaze_____ at the world_____ all___ a -

round. Made a vow_____ that_ some -

how I would find_____ fame__ and for - tune.__

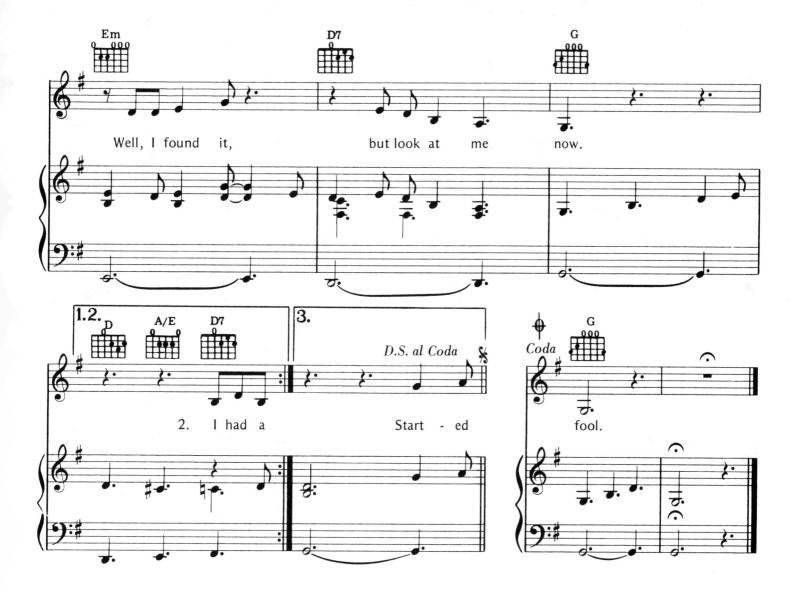

2. I had a sweetheart who would love me forever.
Didn't need her; I would reign all alone.
And look at me; I'm the king of a cold, lonely castle,
And the queen of my heart is gone.

3. Gather 'round me, you fools, for a dollar.
Listen to me, and a lesson you'll learn.
Wealth is happiness and love,
Sent from Heaven above,
And the fires of ambition will burn.

I'D HAVE TO BE CRAZY

Words and Music by
STEVE FROMHOLZ

you. _____ And I'd have to be cra - zy, plumb out of my

mind, to fall out of love with you. _____

2. Now I know I've done weird things
    Told people I heard things
    When silence was all that abound
    Been days when it pleased me
    To be on my knees following ants as they crawled 'cross the ground.
    I been insane on a train
    But I'm still me again
    The place where I hold you is true.
    I know I'm all-right
    'Cause I'd have to be crazy to fall out of love with you.

BRIDGE

3. I sure would be dingy
    To live in an envelope
    Just a-waitin' alone for a stamp
    You'd say I was loco
    If I rubbed for a genie while burning my hand on the lamp.
    I may not be normal
    But nobody is.
    I'd like to say 'fore I'm through
    I'd have to be crazy plumb out of my mind
    To fall out of love with you.
    I'd have to be crazy
    Plumb out of my mind to fall out of love with you.

SEPTEMBER SONG

Words by
MAXWELL ANDERSON

Music by
KURT WEILL

85

MAMMAS DON'T LET YOUR BABIES GROW UP TO BE COWBOYS

Moderate ♩ = 63

Words and Music by
ED BRUCE and
PATSY BRUCE

Cow-boys ain't eas-y to love and they're hard-er to hold.
Cow-boys like smok-y old pool rooms and clear moun-tain morn-ings,

They'd rath-er give you a
lit-tle warm pup-pies and

song than dia-monds or gold.
chil-dren and girls of the night.

TO ALL THE GIRLS I'VE LOVED BEFORE

Lyrics by
HAL DAVID

Music by
ALBERT HAMMOND

loved

be - fore.

blow - ing___ and ev - 'ry time I tried to stay.

The winds of change con - tin - ued blow - ing, and they just car - ried me a -

way. 3. To all the girls we've

GEORGIA ON MY MIND

Words by
STUART GORRELL

Music by
HOAGY CARMICHAEL